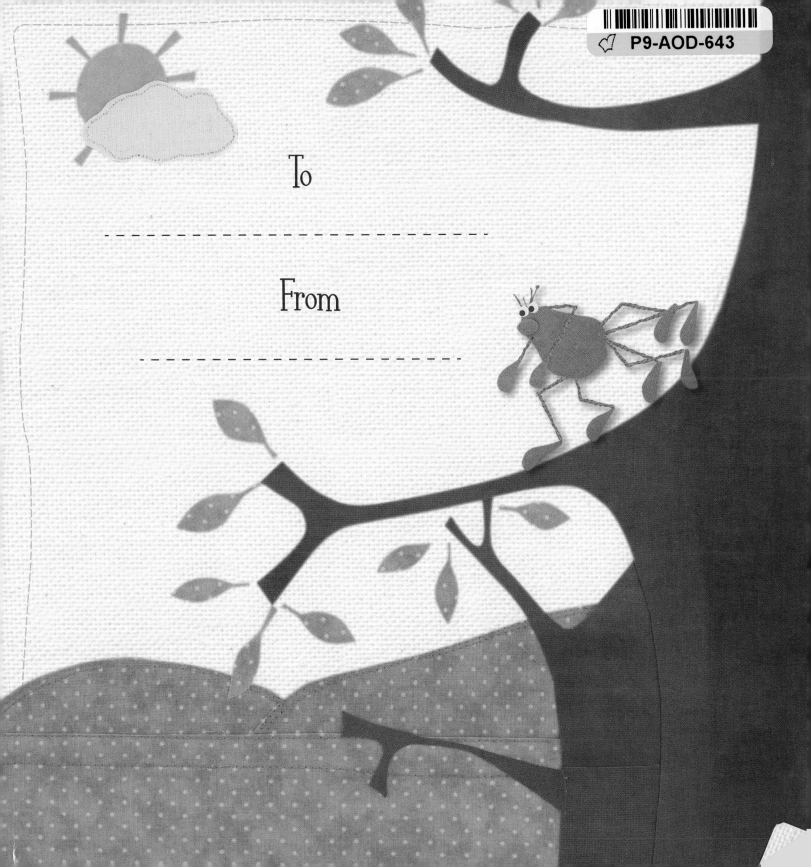

To

- -

From

- -

Itsy Bitsy spider

Kate Toms

make
believe
ideas

Itsy Bitsy
Spider
went UP the waterspout.
DOWN came the rain,
and washed the spider OUT.

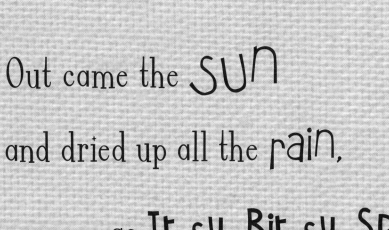

Out came the sun
and dried up all the rain,

so Itsy Bitsy Spider

climbed up the spout again.

Here we go again!

But why does **Itsy** climb the **spout**?

(In case you are in any doubt.)

Because he's **spun** his web up **high**,

so he can **see** the **world** go by . . .

(It's easy **dropping** to the floor,
but climbing **UP** is quite a chore.)

Itsy Bitsy Spider

doesn't like the **rain**,

he's got his **swimming goggles** on,

(he won't get caught again).

But . . . just as he starts climbing UP the waterspout, another shower of rain falls down and washes Itsy out!

Uh-oh!

Looking **around**, what's **Itsy** seen?
A **round** and **bouncy** trampoline!

Wheeeee!

He's found a way to get home **fast** . . .

but bounces high

and flies straight Past...

Not again!

Over the hedge,

over the wall,

a blue striped tent

breaks his fall.

Looking puzzled,

Itsy thinks.

He rubs his hairy head and blinks.

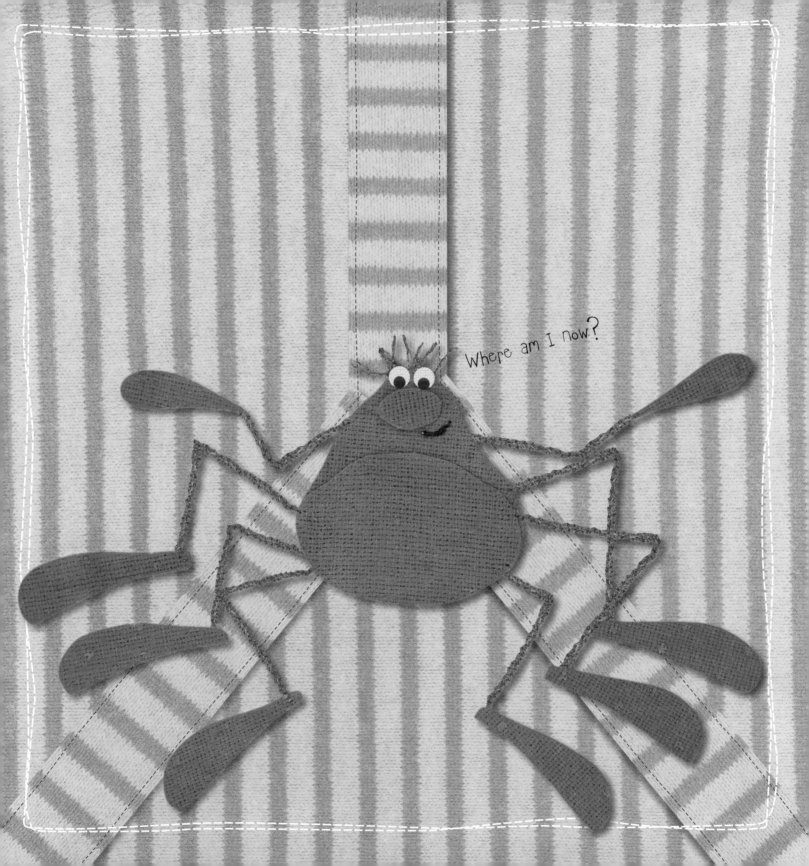

Where am I now?

The wash is **drying,**

the **weather's** fine,

Itsy wobbles on the line,

when suddenly a breezy breeze blows Itsy to some nearby trees.

Through the leaves, **Itsy** spies several pairs of **beady eyes.**

"But **worse** than that," **Itsy** squeaks,

Itsy's running, all puffed out,

but in the distance,

sees the

spout.

It's the best idea
he's had all day.

He'll climb the spout another way.

The rain comes down

inside the spout,

so he'll climb UP

not in, but out!

Back in his web,

he's happy now.

(It's easy when you've worked out how . . .)

The lesson learned?

Don't wear a frown —

even when the rain comes down!

Home at last!

So **Itsy Bitsy Spider** can climb the waterspout.

And even if the **rain pours down**, it can't wash **Itsy** out.

For **Itsy Bitsy Spider** has found **another** way,

and now it's really easy